When 10-year-old Ben Tennyson stumbles upon a mysterious alien device in the woods one summer, little does he realise that his life is set to change - forever.

As soon as the watch-like Omnitrix quite literally gets a grip on him, Ben discovers it gives him the ability to transform into 10 different alien super-beings, each one with awesome powers!

Using the Omnitrix to cause super-powered mischief turns out to be fun, but will Ben learn to use his might to fight for good?

READ ON AND FIND OUT . . .

EGMONT
We bring stories to life

Published in Great Britain 2009
by Egmont UK Limited
239 Kensington High Street, London W8 6SA

Ben 10 and all related characters and elements
are trademarks of and © Cartoon Network.
(s09)

Adapted from the animated series by
Barry Hutchison

1 3 5 7 9 10 8 6 4 2

A CIP catalogue record for this title is available from
the British Library

Printed and bound in Great Britain by the CPI Group

CHAPTER ONE

MANY YEARS AGO . . .

High in the mountains, in the heart of a huge forest, a hidden missile-launching platform slowly began to slide open. Inside, a nuclear warhead – one of the most devastating weapons on the planet – lay motionless.

Suddenly, a blinding beam of yellow light stretched down from above, bathing the missile in its strange, twinkling glow. With a creaking and groaning of metal, the weapon tore free of the platform and began to soar upwards into the dark night sky.

AWOOGA! AWOOGA!

A screeching alarm echoed through the corridors of the missile base. Red light bulbs flashed into life on the grey metal walls, casting a spooky glow over the entire underground complex.

'Security breach!' warned an urgent computer voice. 'Red alert!'

The base commander skidded round the door frame and ran into the command room. A soldier sat at the control desk, anxiously pressing at flashing buttons. On the display screen in front of him, six more missiles shot up from the ground.

'I didn't authorise a launch!' boomed the commander. 'Abort! Abort!'

'We're *not* launching the nukes, sir!' replied the soldier, frantically flicking switches. 'Something's pulling them out of their holders!'

✖ ✖ ✖

With a **WHOOSH**, yet another nuclear missile was dragged from its mooring by the yellow beam. Up, up it went, before being swallowed by a hatch in the bottom of a large, heavily armoured alien battleship.

Three more warheads soared upwards, and three more after that. Each one was quickly pulled into the bowels of the alien ship.

�֍ ✖ ✖

An explosion ripped through the inside of the missile base, tearing a thick metal door from its hinges and filling the area with choking black smoke.

A platoon of armed soldiers stood ready, their weapons trained on the wide hole in the wall. Their fingers twitched on their guns' triggers. It was difficult to see through the smoke, but it looked as if something had moved.

The air hissed as a blast of red-hot energy

erupted from within the cloud. It hit the closest soldier square in the chest, throwing him off his feet. He hit the ground, unconscious.

The other soldiers braced themselves, ready for combat. Before they had a chance to open fire, another round of laser blasts burst through the smoke. In less than a second, they and their guns had clattered noisily on to the metal floor.

Two robotic drones hovered through the black haze, their weapons scanning for any more targets. Following behind them was a hulking brute of an alien. His beard of thick, slimy tentacles twitched as he stalked along the corridor.

He was Vilgax, the most feared creature in the entire known universe.

Vilgax strode across to the nearest nuclear missile and studied it. His mouth curled into a grin, revealing two rows of razor-sharp teeth.

'Primitive,' he growled. 'But destructive enough.'

ZZZZZZZAP!

As the alien finished speaking, a bright-blue laser beam fizzled through the air beside his head, and one of his robotic drones exploded in a spectacular fireball. Vilgax spun round, fists clenched, only for a second bolt of energy to strike him. Its force pushed him backwards, away from the missiles, but otherwise the alien was unhurt.

'You!' he hissed, his eyes narrowed.

A figure stepped from the shadows, his

face hidden by the helmet of his protective suit. He clutched a large rifle, strange lights blinking along its side.

Behind him, a smaller man stepped forwards. Though he was dressed the same, the second man was armed with a sleek handgun. His movements were less confident than those of the first man; he seemed edgy and nervous.

'It's over, Vilgax,' said the first man, his voice strong and commanding.

'You're going down!' chirped his younger-sounding colleague.

Vilgax slowly began to advance on the two men, his fists still tightly clenched.

'Many have tried,' he snarled. 'None have succeeded.'

'Until now, slimeball!' yelled the man with the pistol. He leaped forward, firing wild laser blasts at the alien.

'Phil! Wait!' the first man cried, but it was too late. Vilgax threw himself over the rain of energy beams, and flipped over in mid-air. Phil looked up just in time for the alien's foot to connect with his head. With a thud, his helmet hit the ground.

The first man watched helplessly as Vilgax twisted Phil round and used him as a human shield. In one swift movement, the alien tore the laser pistol from his prisoner's hand. Phil gulped nervously as it was pressed against his head.

Nearby, the second robot drone scuttled over to one of the few remaining nuclear missiles. It inserted a probe spike into the launch controls and began transmitting data. The screen on the controls blinked into life, and the words 'Launch ready' lit up the console.

'Back away,' Vilgax hissed, 'or watch one of your main cities be destroyed!'

The man with the rifle hesitated, his gun still pointed at the monstrous alien. Vilgax pressed his stolen gun harder against the side of Phil's head.

'Put the weapon down,' he barked. 'NOW!'

The man let his rifle clatter to the floor. Vilgax watched as the man kicked it to one side.

'You can't just let him get away!' yelped Phil, struggling against Vilgax's grip.

Beneath his helmet, the man smirked. 'Never said I would, kid.' He threw up his arm and a hidden blaster popped up. A bolt of energy screeched from it, hitting Vilgax before the alien could react.

Stunned, Vilgax released his grip on the gun. Phil aimed a crunching elbow blow backwards into the alien's ribs, and quickly ducked free of his grip.

'You're too late!' Vilgax hissed. Behind him, the nuclear missile roared into life and began to shudder and shake.

'Wrong! My timing's perfect,' corrected the man in the helmet. Stepping forwards, he flicked his rifle up into his hands and fired. A blob of thick, black goo shot from the barrel.

As the stuff hit Vilgax, it expanded and

wrapped round him. The force of the collision knocked him backwards into his robot drone, and the two found themselves glued to the missile by the oily goo.

'NOOOOOO!' Vilgax roared, struggling helplessly as the missile screamed skyward.

'What are you doing?' demanded Phil, as the other man ran across to the control panel and began pressing buttons.

'Sending Vilgax out with a bang!' came the reply.

They looked up through the launch hatch and watched the missile head off course. Just before it collided with Vilgax's ship, the alien let out a loud, bellowing cry: 'TENNYSON!'

High in the mountains, above a huge, sprawling forest, an alien battleship exploded with an ear-shattering *BAD-OOOOM!*

CHAPTER TWO

HAVOCBEAST BY NAME . . .

In the passenger seat of The Rust Bucket, Ben Tennyson's eyes were wide with wonder. His cousin, Gwen, sat at the motorhome's cramped dining table. Both of them were staring at their Grandpa Max in the driving seat. He had just finished telling them how he and his partner, Phil, had once battled Vilgax, and they could hardly believe their ears.

'And then – **KABLAMMO!**' Grandpa continued. 'No more Vilgax.' He glanced across at his grandson. 'Or so I thought.'

'Whoa!' gasped Ben. 'You were a hero!'

Grandpa shook his head. 'I was just a guy doing a job.'

'Excuse me,' asked Gwen, 'but exactly what *was* that job?'

Her grandfather sighed. He'd never told anyone about his old career before, but he was determined to be honest with his grandchildren.

'We called ourselves "The Plumbers",' he began. 'Officially, we didn't exist. We were the guys who fixed the problems no one else could. Extraterrestrial, extrasensory, extraordinary . . .'

'So all this time I've been going hero, I've really been following in your footsteps,' said Ben. He thought about this for a few moments, then grinned. 'I'm a Plumber in training!'

'And you knew about the watch the whole time?' demanded Gwen.

'Not really,' Grandpa assured her. 'Just rumour and scuttlebutt.' He glanced down at the Omnitrix on his grandson's arm. 'I was as surprised as you guys when it turned up on Ben's wrist.'

'You always told us we could tell you anything, Grandpa,' said Gwen. She leaned her head on one hand and stared out of the window. The sun was just beginning to set over the carved stone heads of the world-famous Mount Rushmore. 'Guess you didn't feel the same.'

Before Grandpa could reply, a wailing of sirens split the evening air. Wrenching the wheel, he pulled The Rust Bucket over on to the side of the road as a procession of police cars, fire engines and ambulances thundered by.

'All right!' cried Ben. 'Could be a chance for the Plumbers to go back to work!'

Gwen snorted. 'You should start by unclogging that hairball from your brain, Mr Plumber.'

'You're just jealous cos you're not part of the family business,' Ben replied, turning to stick his tongue out at his cousin.

'There *is* no "family business",' said Grandpa dismissively. 'My hero days were over a long time ago.'

'Well, *mine* are just getting started!' Ben crowed, throwing open the door of The Rust Bucket.

'Ben, wait!' Grandpa Max called, but Ben was already outside, twisting the dial on the Omnitrix. Whenever he needed to get somewhere fast, there was one alien he could always rely on.

'Time to XLR8!'

As Ben slammed his hand down on the

watch, a familiar cloud of green energy wrapped itself round him. Immediately, he began to change. His legs stretched. His arms grew. His feet formed into flippers.

Wait. Flippers?!

'Awww, Ripjaws?' he groaned. 'What a rip *off*!'

There was no way he could run after the police cars now. Still, he'd learned long ago that being a hero sometimes meant making the most of a bad situation.

As a fire engine screamed by, Ripjaws reached out a webbed hand and caught hold of a ladder. Clinging on tightly, he let the speeding vehicle carry him towards the unknown emergency that lay ahead.

�֍ ✖ ✖

Brakes screeching, the emergency vehicles pulled up outside a large hotel. Dozens of well-dressed guests huddled in groups outside, nervously glancing across at the building.

'There's some kind of creature inside!' yelped the hotel manager, as the last of the fire engines arrived on the scene. 'It's tearing up the place!'

He stopped, mid-panic, as a sudden torrent of water began to fall like heavy rain from above. Looking up, the manager gasped with shock. Standing on top of the closest fire engine, Ripjaws was soaking up the spray from the hose he was holding.

'Sorry,' said the alien. 'Just needed to moisturise.'

Without another word, Ripjaws somersaulted down from the roof of the vehicle and landed with a faint **SCHLOP** on the soaking-wet ground. Watched by dozens of startled onlookers, he sprinted over to the hotel's double doors and pushed them open.

Splintered furniture lay everywhere. Articles of luggage were scattered across the floor, most of them torn wide open. Clothes spilled from within the damaged cases, and those too were ripped to shreds. Of everything in the lobby, only two stone pillars and an impressive marble fountain remained intact.

'OK,' demanded Ripjaws, stepping in and letting the doors swing closed behind him. 'Who's the punk giving us "creatures" a bad name?'

A low, rumbling groan echoed around the lobby. A savage-looking alien known as a Havocbeast stepped from the shadows, snapping at the air with its pincer-like claws. Its eyes burned a dark, ominous red, and from its mouth hung long, thick strands of extraterrestrial drool.

Ripjaws blinked and peered down at the Havocbeast. The Havocbeast, in turn, looked up at him. And up. And up, until it almost fell over backwards.

The tiny alien snarled as Ripjaws roared with laughter. He could hardly believe that so

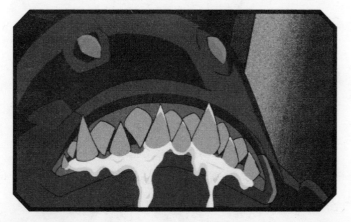

much destruction could be caused by something barely bigger than a basketball!

The Havocbeast snatched a lump of rubble from the ruined lobby floor and launched it at Ripjaws, smacking him hard in the head

Ripjaws glared at the little creature. 'You picked the wrong day to be an alien, pal!'

He launched himself at the Havocbeast, arms outstretched, ready to scoop up the tiny critter. Too late!

THUD! Ripjaws landed hard on the spot where the creature had stood. From high up on the nearest stone pillar, it was the Havocbeast's turn to laugh. Its strange, high-pitched snigger only made Ripjaws angrier.

The Havocbeast threw itself from the pillar. Curling up into a ball, it landed in the ornamental fountain with a **SPLOSH**. It quickly popped back up, its cheeks bulging.

SQUIRT! The miniature alien giggled happily as it spat a mouthful of water in Ripjaws' face. Ben's alien form absorbed the liquid into his scaly skin, drawing strength from it as he watched the Havocbeast scurry away.

'That's just a breath of fresh air to me,' he said, before setting off in pursuit of the tiny terror.

� ✤ ✤

Outside the hotel, a motorhome coughed and spluttered into the car park. Before the engine had shuddered to a stop, The Rust Bucket's doors flew open, and Grandpa and Gwen dashed out.

When she spotted the manager, Gwen stopped, scratched her head and asked, 'Did anyone happen to see a giant talking fish come by here?'

✤ ✤ ✤

Back inside the building, Ripjaws crept along the corridors, searching for any trace of the Havocbeast.

Edging backwards, he scanned the shadows for movement. Halfway down a corridor, he bumped into something large. Spinning on the spot, he came face to face with a middle-aged man holding a very big gun.

'Aaargh! Who are you?' they both cried at once. 'Who am I?' they each demanded. 'Who are *you*?'

With a shrug, the man suddenly raised his weapon and fired. The blast sent Ripjaws sprawling along the floor. He thudded to a stop against a wall.

The armed man stepped forwards, his rifle raised. Strange lights blinked along its side as he took aim at Ripjaws.

'Looks like today's my lucky day,' he sneered. 'Two aliens for the price of one!'

CHAPTER THREE

AN OLD FRIEND

Ripjaws groaned as he tried to sit up. The blast had taken a lot out of him. If he could only rest for a few moments, he'd be fine.

But the man with the gun wasn't about to give him time to recover. He stepped closer to Ripjaws, the rifle aimed at the hero's head.

A sudden inhuman roar made the man whip round. The Havocbeast was approaching, its tiny arms stretched out, ready to attack. The gunman's protective body armour creaked as he craned his neck to look down at Ripjaws.

'Just sit tight, fishstick,' he spat. 'I'll be back in a minute.'

The Havocbeast screamed and ran for

its life as a burst of laser fire scorched the floor around it. Grinning, the gunman set off firing wildly.

Slowly, his arms shaking from the effort, Ripjaws reached up and pulled a jug of iced water down from the desk above his head. The cool, clear liquid poured down on him, instantly giving him a recharge.

'Ahhh,' he sighed. 'You've got to love room service!'

Not far off, the armed man crept cautiously along the corridor, searching for any sign of the Havocbeast. The alien was small and fast, but it couldn't hide forever.

Suddenly, a high bookcase began to wobble back and forth. Too late to run, the man threw up his arms for protection as hundreds of books rained down on top of him, followed by the heavy wooden book case itself – **THUMP!**

The Havocbeast leaped down from the fallen shelves and danced with delight.

As it celebrated, a large metal safe clanked down over it, trapping it. It banged angrily against the walls of its prison, but they were too strong to break.

'Not bad for a fishstick, huh?' said Ripjaws, watching the man struggle beneath the bookcase.

Before he could decide whether to help him or not, the Omnitrix began to flash red. **BLEEP BLEEP BLEEP BLEEEEP!** In the blink of an eye, Ripjaws transformed back to plain old Ben. Luckily, the gunman hadn't seen the change, and Ben was able to leave the scene before the man could pull himself free.

He was running so fast he almost smacked straight into Grandpa Max, who was standing with Gwen just inside the hotel doorway.

'Ben, are you all right?'

'Barely!' cried Ben. 'Some nutjob in there nearly roasted me!' He glanced back along the corridor just as the armed man dragged himself free of the shelves. The man's eyes almost popped out of his head when he spotted Grandpa.

'Max!' he gasped.

A broad grin spread across Grandpa's face. 'Phil!' he said, beaming.

Ben watched on, shocked, as the two old friends hugged warmly.

'You *know* this guy, Grandpa?'

'You could say that,' said Phil, nodding. 'We used to be partners.'

Ben glanced across at Gwen. This day was just full of surprises.

❊ ❊ ❊

With a grunt of effort, Phil heaved the heavy safe into the back of his worn-out old car, the Havocbeast thudding against the inside.

The metal box safely tucked in the boot, Phil gave the car a loving pat. 'Yeah,' he admitted, catching Grandpa's stare, 'she's not much to look at, but she's better than that old rust bucket of a motorhome you used to drive.'

Grandpa smiled and quickly changed the subject. 'So, how are you?'

'Pretty good considering I just bagged a Havocbeast. Seems like old times.'

'*You* bagged it?' Ben snapped. 'As if! It was Rip–'

Grandpa stepped in front of Ben before he could give too much away. 'Havocbeast, huh?' he said quickly. 'Haven't seen one of those since the one we caught terrorising Denver years ago.'

'Yeah, well, good thing I was around,'

said Phil, smiling. 'You know, once a Plumber, always a Plumber.' His eyes lit up as he had an idea. 'Ever think about getting back in the game, Max? You know, relive the glory days?'

'No, thanks, I'm retired,' replied Grandpa. 'And so are the Plumbers.'

'Yeah, thanks to you,' Phil said. 'Once you took Vilgax out of the picture, the work just seemed to dry up.'

'Just doing my job.' Grandpa shrugged.

'Yeah . . . anyway,' continued Phil, 'looks like things are picking back up again. In fact, I'm starting my own freelance Plumber business . . .' He trailed off when he saw Ben's wrist. 'Wow!' He whistled, his eyes narrowing. 'Cool watch. It looks so familiar . . .'

'It should,' explained Ben. 'It's the Omni–'

'Look at the time!' Grandpa said loudly. He caught Ben by the shoulder and began to shove him in the direction of The Rust Bucket. 'We need to go. Nice catching up with you, Phil. Happy Plumbing!'

❊ ❊ ❊

The Rust Bucket rattled along a darkened highway, Grandpa behind the wheel. Ben sat up front, feet on the dashboard, hands behind his head. He looked at his grandpa, confused.

'I don't get it,' he said. 'How come you didn't tell Phil about the Omnitrix?'

'That's on a need-to-know basis only, Ben. The fewer people who know, the better.'

'Guess that's your answer to everything, isn't it, Grandpa?' muttered Gwen from somewhere in the back.

'Hey, why don't we start up the Plumbers again?' asked Ben excitedly. 'You, me and Phil. We'd be super alien-butt kickers!'

Grandpa sighed and shook his head. 'Ben, I'm flattered you appreciate what I did, but you can't bring back the past.'

Ben opened his mouth to argue, but a sound from The Rust Bucket's dashboard stopped him. With a faint **BLEEP**, a screen slid out from beneath the instrument panel. It hissed noisily, before blinking into life.

Phil stared out of it. He spoke, his voice urgent and desperate.

'Max, if you're out there, I need help,' he begged. 'Two Vulpimancers are tearing up a meat-processing plant on Highway Forty-four!'

Grandpa's breath caught in his throat. 'Vulpimancers?' he muttered. This wasn't good.

Grandpa heaved the motorhome round and sped off towards Highway Forty-four.

'All right!' cried Ben as he was bounced around in his seat. 'The Tennysons are back in the Plumbing business!'

※ ※ ※

From the outside, the meat-processing plant looked just like any other warehouse – even if it didn't sound like one. Savage alien roars tore out through the shattered doors and into the night, as Grandpa, Ben and Gwen stepped down from The Rust Bucket.

'I don't like the sound of that,' said Gwen, shivering. Grandpa moved past her and silently led the way into the darkened building.

The air inside the plant was icy cold. Their breath formed clouds as Grandpa and the two cousins crept along the main corridor where rows of meat hung down from giant hooks.

At the end of the corridor, they found Phil. He was kneeling down by one of the hanging lumps of meat, clutching his ribs.

'Max!' he cried when he saw the approaching Tennysons. 'Thank goodness you showed up. Two aliens. Nasty.' He grinned. 'We're going to need a little of that old magic!'

'No worries,' said Ben, nodding. He ran his fingers over the Omnitrix. 'We're on it.'

CRASH! A nearby metal door slammed to the floor, releasing freezing clouds of air into the corridor. As the clouds cleared, two huge shapes clambered through on all fours.

These aliens looked a lot like one of Ben's – the savage Wildmutt – but they were bigger, stronger and more ferocious. They caught the scent of the humans and roared.

Gwen gulped nervously and gave her cousin a nudge. 'Friends of yours?'

CHAPTER FOUR

DOGFIGHT

Ben spun the dial on the Omnitrix.

'Vulpinancers,' he muttered. 'Maybe I can talk to them.'

'Ben!' Grandpa began, but the green energy was already swirling round his grandson, changing him.

'*That's* why I recognise that watch,' said Phil in amazement. 'It's the Omnitrix!'

As soon as he had fully transformed, Wildmutt leaped in front of the oncoming Vulpimancers. They stopped and bared their huge fangs at the tiny runt before them.

Unable to actually speak Vulpimancer, Ben gave a low whine and hoped that it meant something friendly. The beasts seemed to listen for a few moments, before the largest threw back its head and bellowed angrily.

'Vulpimancers never were big on small,' Grandpa said with a gulp.

He watched helplessly as the two Vulpimancers lunged at Wildmutt. The smaller alien turned and fled through the processing plant, but his two bigger cousins set off after him, snapping at his heels.

Faster and faster Wildmutt ran. He could smell the two mega-mutts getting closer and closer. He could feel their heavy footsteps shaking the room. Any minute now one of them was sure to pounce.

Right on cue, the largest Vulpimancer threw itself forwards. Wildmutt was ready. Leaping upwards, he caught the chain of a dangling meat hook and swung out of the beast's reach. Its sharp claws clacked wildly as it skidded across the floor, unable to stop.

Flailing frantically, the Vulpimancer crashed into a stack of barrels. All four of them toppled, spilling a mound of smelly animal guts down over the savage alien's hairy head.

But Wildmutt wasn't out of danger yet! The second Vulpimancer caught the bottom of the chain he was dangling from and gave it a firm yank. With a creaking of metal, the chain links snapped, and Wildmutt found himself tumbling towards the ground.

Twisting his body, Wildmutt landed on a moving conveyor belt. The mega-mutt slammed hard into him, knocking him on to his back.

Then the bigger beast leaped on him, pinning him in place. Wildmutt howled. The moving platform was leading them towards a mincing machine! If he couldn't escape, he was going to end up as alien burger-meat!

Close by, Phil pressed random buttons on the plant's control panel. Lights flashed and machinery whirred into life.

A split second before Wildmutt was dragged into the spinning blades of the mincer, the conveyor belt shuddered to a stop. With a push of a lever, Phil sent a heavy hunk of meat slamming into the Vulpimancer's side. The alien yelped as it was sent spinning through the air.

Wildmutt leaped down from the platform, landing next to Phil.

'What are partners for?' The man grinned. Wildmutt nodded his thanks, and the two of them – along with Gwen and Grandpa – made a dash for the exit.

Before they could reach safety, the first Vulpimancer stepped into their path. They all turned, ready to retreat, only to find the second alien stalking up behind them. Gwen stared at the beast's enormous fangs and gasped.

'Don't suppose you've ever considered becoming a vegetarian?' she quipped.

Suddenly, a piercing squeal vibrated through the factory. Wildmutt and the Vulpimancers all dropped to the floor, howling in pain as the sound attacked their super-sensitive hearing.

'Sorry about that, Ben,' said Phil, holding

up the device emitting the high-pitched sound. 'Only way to bring down a Vulpimancer.'

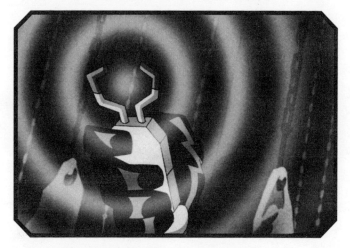

Grandpa eyed the contraption suspiciously. 'Yeah,' he muttered, 'lucky for us you had a sonic pitch whistle with you.'

BLEEP BLEEP BLEEP BLEEEEP! The Omnitrix suddenly began to flash. Where Wildmutt had stood there was now only Ben, still clutching his aching ears.

'So, all the stories are true,' drawled Phil, 'the Omnitrix really does exist.' He grinned down at Ben. 'Pretty good moves out there. You remind me of your grandfather back in the day.'

'Really?' asked Ben, his eyes wide with wonder.

Behind Phil, one of the Vulpimancers screeched with rage.

'Look out!' cried Grandpa Max, but the warning came too late. The alien swatted the sonic weapon from Phil's hand. As the whistle shattered against the far wall, the factory once again fell silent.

In a split second, the mega-mutts rounded on Phil, hot alien drool dripping from their jagged teeth. This was one meal they were going to enjoy!

'Why don't you pick on someone with more meat on his bones!' boomed Grandpa Max. The aliens turned just in time for a fork-lift truck to thunder into them. Grandpa pushed the accelerator pedal to the floor, steering the beasts towards the open door of a wide, walk-in freezer.

Just before the forklift passed through the door, Grandpa jumped off. Hitting the ground with a thud, he quickly rolled upright and hit the door's 'close' button. With a mechanical hiss, the metal door swung into place, trapping the aliens inside.

'Just like old times, eh?' Phil smiled. 'I think this is going to be the beginning of a new partnership!'

✹ ✹ ✹

Back at Phil's hotel room, Ben was munching his way through the entire contents of the room-service trolley. This was *way* better than his grandfather's cooking!

'Ritzy suite!' Grandpa Max whistled, taking in the lavish surroundings. 'Had to cost a pretty penny.'

Phil leaned back in his chair and shrugged. 'Just a little "thank you" I negotiated for helping the manager out with his alien problem. And trust me –' he winked – 'this is just the tip of the iceberg.'

'Y'know, Ben,' he continued, 'you'd make a great Plumber.'

'I would?'

'Sure! A real chip off the old block. We'd make a great team. With your powers, Max's experience and my instincts, we'd be unstoppable!' He turned to Grandpa. 'What do you think?'

'I'm thinking,' began Grandpa, scratching his chin, 'what an odd coincidence for a Havocbeast and two Vulpimancers to turn up on the same day.'

'Aliens,' said Phil with a shrug. 'Go figure.'

Grandpa stared long and hard at Phil, then turned and headed for the door. 'I need some fresh air.'

Phil watched the door slam through

narrowed eyes. His old partner was up to something. But what?

'Hey, kids,' he said, opening the door again, 'order whatever you'd like off the room-service menu.'

'Now we're talking!' Ben replied, but Phil had already slipped outside.

'Something's going on that Grandpa's not telling us about.' Gwen frowned. She stood up and went to follow Phil. 'Come on.'

'And pass up free room service?' Ben spluttered. 'No way, I'm staying here!'

'You're right,' said Gwen slyly. 'It's probably just some secret Plumber mission. Better if we just stay out of it.'

Ben paused, mid-bite. Secret Plumber mission, eh? He liked the sound of that.

❈ ❈ ❈

The wind whipped through the empty car park

as Ben and Gwen stepped out through the hotel
doors.

'No Grandpa,' said Gwen

'And no Phil,' added Ben. 'But where
would they go?'

Gwen glanced around. From here she
could see all the way down into the nearest
town, and all the way up to Mount Rushmore.
During their last encounter with Vilgax,
Grandpa had shown her an underground vault
hidden inside the mountain.

'If Grandpa thinks that little alien weasel

and those space mutts are connected, there's only one place around here to check out!'

❖ ❖ ❖

A concealed door clanked open beneath the giant stone head of George Washington, and Grandpa stepped into an old Plumber base. It stood empty and silent, its occupants long since gone.

Almost immediately, Grandpa Max's worst fears were confirmed. The Null Void Projector – the Plumbers' single most powerful weapon – had been removed from its case.

'Looking for this?'

Grandpa turned to find Phil standing in the doorway, the weapon held tightly in his hand.

'The Null Void Projector.' Grandpa scowled. 'I knew those aliens were familiar. You stole the projector to release the ones we caught back in the old days!'

'You always were too smart for your own good, Max.' Phil smirked. 'But not wanting to join up with me was just plain dumb.'

'Why are you doing all this?' Grandpa demanded.

'Job security. I release an alien, then get some hotel manager or mayor or whoever to pay me to catch it. Easy money.'

'I'm not going to let you get away with this!'

'Yeah, I figured you might say that.' Phil flipped a switch and the Null Void Projector hummed into life. 'Too bad. We could've made quite a team again.'

A thin beam of yellow energy shot out of the weapon, and Grandpa threw himself to the ground. He looked up to see a large portal tearing open just a few metres away.

The hole in space rippled and grew as a huge, monstrous creature pushed its way through. The green-skinned beast snarled, revealing hundreds of gleaming, saw-like teeth. It scuttled forward on four long legs, each one of which ended with a razor-sharp clawed foot.

Grandpa stared, frozen to the spot in horror, as the orc-like creature turned on him and moved in for the kill!

CHAPTER FIVE

TRAITOR!

The hulking alien raised one of its deadly claws and aimed a blow at Grandpa Max. A split second before it hit, a black-and-blue blur whipped through the bunker. The orc's foot cracked the rock where Grandpa had been.

It screeched as it realised its leg was stuck fast.

Phil spluttered. 'What the –?'

Across the room, XLR8 skidded to a halt, Grandpa held safely in his arms.

'You're no Plumber,' he told Phil. 'You're nothing but a big drip!'

'Ben, listen to me,' the traitor begged. 'We don't need your grandpa. We could start the Plumbers back up again, just you and me!'

'Forget it,' XLR8 scoffed, setting his grandfather down. 'And there's nothing you can do to change my mind.'

'Sorry to hear that,' sighed Phil, backing towards the door. His eyes lit up as the hulking green alien finally tore its foot free of the rock. 'Say hello to an old friend,' he cried. 'A Wigzellian Orc Beast!'

The creature swung wildly, its massive claws swiping the air by Grandpa Max's head. XLR8 caught Grandpa by the arm and dragged him out of harm's way. He sped towards the metal security door, but Phil slammed it closed behind him, trapping the heroes inside.

XLR8 shot off to battle the Orc Beast. He dodged and weaved past its flailing claws, before landing a hundred punches in less than a second. The Orc Beast barely flinched, launching a counter-attack, which XLR8 only just dodged.

At the far end of the chamber, Grandpa slid open a hidden drawer. Reaching inside, he pulled out a weird mechanical object shaped like a mini-umbrella.

'No,' he muttered, replacing the item and opening other drawers. None of them held what he was looking for.

'Grandpa, could you pick up the pace?' scowled XLR8, dodging another frenzied attack. Behind him, the Orc Beast tore up a large section of floor and took aim. XLR8 rose up on the balls of his feet, ready to speed out of danger, but –

BLEEP BLEEP BLEEP BLEEEEP!

With a red flash from the Omnitrix, XLR8 reverted back to Ben. The chunk of flooring hit him on the chest, knocking him over and pinning him below its weight.

'Got it!' Grandpa cried. He pulled a polished silver hand grenade from a drawer and lobbed it towards the Orc Beast. As it connected with the bulky alien, a cloud of green gas hissed from within its metal casing.

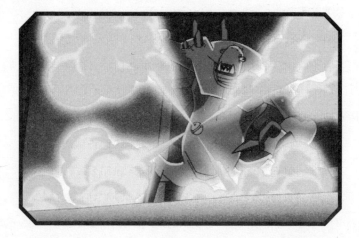

Groaning, the creature slumped to the ground, unconscious. Grandpa ran across to his grandson and helped him out from beneath the rubble. The pair dusted themselves down and looked around the chamber. A horrible realisation suddenly struck them both.

'Where's Gwen?'

✖ ✖ ✖

At that moment, Gwen was crouching down low in the back of Phil's car, wondering what she'd got herself into. She'd overheard him in the Plumber base, and decided it would be a good idea to follow him. Now she wasn't so sure.

'Who says crime doesn't pay?' Phil chuckled. He sat the Null Void Projector down on the front passenger seat and turned the key in the car's ignition. The battered old vehicle roared as Phil sped off down the mountain track.

Grandpa and Ben emerged from the chamber just as Phil's dust cloud disappeared down the mountainside. They leaped into The Rust Bucket and set off in pursuit. Phil's car was smaller and faster than the motorhome though. They had no chance of catching up. Or did they?

At the flick of a switch, jet turbo engines unfolded from the motorhome. Ben was thrown back into his seat as The Rust Bucket shot off at what felt like the speed of sound.

Somewhere up ahead, Gwen made a grab for the Null Void Projector.

'Oh no you don't!' Phil snarled, but Gwen was too fast. She yanked the weapon into the back and began to wind down the window.

'Better start thinking of a new line of

work,' she warned, 'because this thing is going bye-bye!'

Phil slammed his hand against the centre of his steering wheel. At once a robotic voice chimed: 'Autopilot engaged.'

The villain clambered into the back as the car continued along the twisty road. Gwen kicked out at him, desperately trying to keep him from the Null Void Projector. As she struggled, the device began to hum. A shimmering portal appeared in the air behind the car.

'Good idea,' smirked Phil as he caught sight of The Rust Bucket tearing along the road behind them. 'We could use a distraction.'

A howling winged creature exploded through the portal and made straight for the first thing it saw – The Rust Bucket. Huge, slimy tentacles wrapped round the front of the vehicle, making it almost impossible for Grandpa to see.

'We need some muscle to stop this thing,' Ben cried, adjusting the Omnitrix. '*Four arms* of muscle!'

A blinding flash of green light illuminated the inside of the motorhome. Grandpa glanced at Ben's seat. A tiny bug-eyed alien sat there, blinking in confusion.

'Grey Matter?' the little extra-terrestrial cried. 'I said *muscle*, not *miniscule*!'

Although small in size, Grey Matter was big in the brains department, and he soon had an idea. Scampering up one of the sticky tentacles, he leaped on to the winged creature's back and pulled at flaps of its saggy skin.

'Triggering the correct series of synapses should allow me some rudimentary motor control . . .' he muttered to himself. The part of him that was still Ben shook his head. 'Sure wish I knew what I was talking about.'

With a stamp of his tiny foot, Grey Matter struck just the right nerve on the flying beast's back. It dropped The Rust Bucket and began to swoop after the speeding car ahead.

CRASH! The full weight of the winged alien smacked down on top of Phil's vehicle, sending it into a wild skid. With a **BANG**, it collided with the metal guard rail at the edge of the road, and came to a shuddering stop.

The abrupt halt sent Grey Matter tumbling from the winged beast's back. He bounced hard on the road next to the car, just as Phil came spilling out. Grey Matter raised his head to find himself staring down the barrel of

the Null Void Projector.

'Back off, small fry,' Phil growled. 'Or I'll release every alien in this thing!'

'Then you'll be out of a job.'

'It doesn't have to be this way,' Phil pleaded. 'We could all work together.'

'No way,' Grey Matter spat. 'This is one hero who's not for sale!'

'Well then, you're all going to be very busy!'

Inside the car, Gwen tore down the rear view mirror and threw it to her cousin, just as Phil fired the projector. Grey Matter caught it and held it up. It reflected the bright yellow beam, engulfing Phil in a shimmering light.

Phil opened his mouth to scream, but before the sound could emerge, he was gone – sucked forever into the Null Void.

'See ya!' cried Gwen.

Grey Matter smiled. 'And I definitely wouldn't want to be ya!'

Back inside the secret Plumber base, Grandpa Max shut the Null Void Projector inside its case. The aliens Phil had released had all been taken care of and everything – for the moment – was back to normal.

'I'm sorry I had to keep my past secret for so long,' Grandpa said. 'I should've known that I could trust you guys.'

'It's OK.' Gwen shrugged.

'And for what it's worth, Ben, you would've made a great Plumber.' He wrapped his arms round his grandchildren. 'Both of you.'

'Hey, we're your grandkids. What do you expect?' beamed Gwen. She glanced at the Null Void Projector. 'What about Phil?'

Grandpa turned and headed for the door, ushering Gwen and Ben out before him. 'I think there are some things in this job we're better off not knowing,' he said.

BEN 10 BOOK COLLECTION

HAVE YOU SEEN THEM ALL?

Ben 10 Alien Force Annual 2010	978 1 4052 4653 8; £7.99
Ben 10 Alien Force colour storybook 1 (Ben 10 Returns Part 1/Part 2)	978 1 4052 4799 3; £4.99
Ben 10 Alien Force colour storybook 2 (The Gauntlet/Be-Knighted)	978 1 4052 4800 6; £4.99
Ben 10 Amazing 3D Hero Vision	978 1 4052 4413 8; £3.99
Ben 10 Puzzle and Quiz Book	978 1 4052 4492 3; £3.99
Ben 10 Magnet Book	978 1 4052 4599 9; £5.99
Ben 10 All Action Stories & Flicker Book	978 1 4052 4512 8; £4.99
Ben 10 comic book 1 (And Then There Were 10)	978 1 4052 4663 7; £4.99
Ben 10 comic book 2 (Washington B.C.)	978 1 4052 4664 4; £4.99
Ben 10 comic book 3 (The Krakken)	978 1 4052 4804 4; £4.99

Ben 10 comic book 4 **(Permanent Retirement)**	978 1 4052 4805 1; £4.99
Ben 10 chapter storybook 1 **(And Then There Were 10/Kevin 11)**	978 1 4052 4467 1; £3.99
Ben 10 chapter storybook 2 **(The Alliance/Secrets)**	978 1 4052 4468 8; £3.99
Ben 10 chapter storybook 3 **(Truth/Framed)**	978 1 4052 4672 9; £4.99
Ben 10 chapter storybook 4 **(The Galactic Enforcers/Ultimate Weapon)**	978 1 4052 4673 6; £4.99

COMING SOON ...
3 COOL NEW BEN 10 BOOKS!

Ben 10 Alien Force Extreme (Pop-Up)	978 1 4052 4852 5; £14.99
Ben 10 Alien Force chapter storybook 1 **(All That Glitters/Max Out)**	978 1 4052 5006 1; £4.99
Ben 10 Alien Force chapter storybook 2 **(Paradox/Plumbers' Helpers)**	978 1 4052 5007 8; £4.99

Visit Egmont.co.uk